THE STORY OF AUTUMN

This book belongs to _____

Who is _____ **years of age.**

THE STORY OF AUTUMN

hard copy   ISBN 978-1-7320197-0-6

soft copy   ISBN 978-1-7320197-2-0

e-book   ISBN 978-1-7320197-0-3

audio book ISBN 978-1-7320197-3-7

copyright © 2017 by Anne E. Reardon

Library of Congress Control Number 1-5969292594

First Edition

written by: Anne E. Reardon

ACKNOWLEDGMENTS

To my children Bob and Kim, the original inspiration for the story many years ago.

I have so many wonderful people who help me stay focused.
To all of you wonderful friends, I thank you from the bottom of my heart.

To my life long friend Sheila Chaps. Thanks for your help.
I will always be in your debt. I am so lucky that you are still in my life.

To Dotty for taking time out of her vacation with family to do the final edit
So appreciate your time.

To Margie, who pointed me in the right direction and did the things I just could not. Without you there would be no covers for this book!
Thank you so much.

Last but by no means least,
to Sue Lovering from Vermont, my best bud! Sue is the one who found the beautiful MapleTree (seen on the back page of this book), she searched and searched to find the perfect Autumn Maple.
Once again I thank you for so many wonderful years of friendship.

DEDICATION

TO ALL THE WONDERFUL YOUNG PEOPLE IN MY LIFE,

THANK YOU FOR YOUR INSPIRATION.

CONTENTS   PAGE

THE WEED   1

SKIPPY   6

MOVING IN   12

A NEW FOREST   16

CONSIDERATION NOT SPITE   21

THE DECISION   25

ACCEPTANCE   31

SUCCESS   38

AUTUMN FOREVER   42

THE WEED

There was a time long, long, long ago when the whole earth was covered with great evergreen forests. There were huge Hemlock, Spruce, Pine, Fir trees, and many more evergreens. It seemed as far as the eye could see, if there were not water or mountains, there was some kind of evergreen tree. One day, deep in the middle of a forest in America, a strange little tree began to grow. The evergreen trees watched this odd young thing with great curiosity. "What do you suppose it is?" asked the huge Blue Spruce.

"Oh, it must be some kind of new weed." said the Pine. " It won't grow much... they never do. The Wind probably dropped some seed to be his bratty old self. One season at the most, that's all any of them last. Judging by how scrawny it is, it won't even last that long. Can you believe that even a weed can be so ugly?" They all agreed, whatever this thing was, by far it was the ugliest thing they had ever seen!

The next few years came and went, however, and the ugly little 'weed' was still there and growing by leaps and bounds! Now, this was becoming a serious situation. The evergreens prided themselves on their appearance and wonderful form. Right here in the middle of them was this gangly thing growing out of control with no shape or real form to it! Its limbs were going in all different directions and worse than that, the limbs

weren't even the same size! What on earth was it? What was it doing

in their pristine forest?

"My goodness!" exclaimed the Spruce one day. "That certainly is a large

weed and, it seems to me, it has been here quite some time! Did you

ask the Wind where he got it? It is definitely getting stronger, not weaker,

and look at it, so straggly and unruly. Why, it has no grace at all with those

bumpy limbs spreading in every direction. It simply has no shape. It

doesn't even stand up straight! It obviously has no grace. What a terrible

thing to have to look at . This thing in our midst will bring shame to our

fine, proud forest. Just wait until the Wind sees it's still here, he will

tell all forest everywhere, that this thing is growing in OUR forest!

We will be the laughing stock everywhere! Whatever are we going to do?"

"I think we should crowd it a bit." said the Pine tree. "It looks as

though if we do it now we are still large enough to weaken it, and maybe it

will just wither and be gone."

"Get close to that horrible thing!? Never," said the Arborvitae.

"I have a better idea," said the Spruce. "Let's call the Wind. After all,

I'm sure he started this mess. We'll ask him to get all the Breezes together and blow the ugly thing down. He will have had his fun and we will be done with it.”

“NO!” said the huge Balsam very loudly. He was by far the most stately and proud tree in the forest. “I don’t think it becomes any of us to even spend time thinking about this weed at all! It’s just too pathetic to look at, never mind cause it harm.”

“Well, of course, that’s the whole point, We don’t want to have to look at it.” spoke the Pine in a testy voice.

“Listen to me” said the Balsam quite forcefully. “It is beneath us to even bother with it. I think we should just ignore it, even though it is growing quite large. That way we avoid shame and, we won’t give the Wind the satisfaction of thinking we care at all. We will just pretend it isn’t even there and, if the Wind says anything about it, we will just act surprised. Then no one will make fun of us but just be curious and talk to us about it. Our reply must be unanimous. We will all say... We really don’t pay attention to it. It must be some kind of weed and is certain to die out.”

So it was decided. All the trees in the forest would ignore the strange thing growing amongst them.

When the young tree heard what they were planning she was crushed.

She had tried so hard to not offend. She never spoke because she was never spoken to. She was so polite she never even thought of interrupting a conversation. All this time she had heard all the terrible things the evergreens said about her. She hoped that by remaining quiet and showing them respect, they would see her as no threat to their forest. She wanted to be no trouble at all. To hear them agree to never have anything to do with her made her so sad. She was hoping by being quiet would earn their friendship. However she was wrong, and she began to cry. She didn't understand why they were being so unkind! How could they dislike her just because she didn't look like them? They had no idea what type of thought process she had. They had never spoken to her! They never gave her a chance and, by the sounds of it, they were never going to.

Skippy, a small, mischievous squirrel who also lived in the great forest, heard the tree crying and jumped over to see what was the going on.

"Hey Ugly, what are you crying about?" asked Skippy.

The tree was so surprised to be spoken to she stopped crying.

"My name is not Ugly," said the tree, "and I'm crying because I found out today that I will always be alone here...that the other trees will never

DRAW OR PASTE A PICTURE OF

YOUR WEED

be my friends. I'm lonely and hurt. I want so much to be friends with the evergreens but they just ignore me no matter how hard I try to impress them with good manners. Just because I look different from them (she pointed one of her bumpy limbs toward the evergreens) they won't have anything do with me!"

"Well Ug,......I mean ah, what is your name?" asked Skippy.

"It's, um...I oughta um...(sniff) I oughta um,..(sniff). Oh, I don't know what it is! No one but you has ever called me anything! Ugly is just not what I want to be called!" Now she was really crying because she didn't even have a name! Skippy, though full of mischief, really had a soft heart and felt so sorry for this tree who just didn't fit in this forest.

"Yeah, you definitely gotta um, have a name. Hey! I've got it! Your name will be Autumn! Short for Oughta Um! What do you think? I think it's kind of cute," said Skippy with a smile.

"Autumn...Autumn...I like the sound of it. What does it mean?" asked the tree.

"What does it mean? Why, ah, it means a great tree with strong limbs. Yeah, that's what it means," said Skippy nervously. "It isn't the name of a weed. It's a great name for a tree! I declare this to be your name and you are definitely a tree."

"Then it's settled, my name is Autumn. I really like that! What does forest

call you?"

"I'm a squirrel to the forest, to you I'm Skippy. All my friends call me

Skippy."

"Your friends? So you will consider me one of your friends?" asked

Autumn. She was so surprised by this that she completely stopped crying.

She was starting to feel better. Here she was, finally having a real

conversation with a squirrel who might become a friend!

"Sure," said Skippy, "and don't let those evergreens get to you. They

don't talk to anyone but each other...they're all stuck up. I run and jump

from one to the other and that really gets them going. They are afraid I

might get one of their branches dirty. I have to go fast 'cause I don't want

to get the sticky stuff that they drip all over the ground on me. Besides,

their needles will prick you if you're not careful. Hey watch this!"

With that , Skippy leaped onto the nearest pine and jumped from one

evergreen to another as fast as he could, and the sight was something to

see! The trees began to shake and shout and call Skippy names. Some

tried to duck so he would miss them but Skippy ran through every tree in a huge circle until he bounded back breathless and laughing to Autumn. "Just

look at them!" Skippy said between breaths and laughter, watching the

chaos he had caused among the evergreens. Soon Autumn too, began to

laugh at the sight of the jiggling trees.

"Oh my," she said, "I shouldn't be laughing at them, but they are so very

funny when they wiggle like that!"

"Hey!" said Skippy, "You look much better when you're not crying. Even

your needles are looking better. I have never in my life seen needles like

yours. May I touch one?"

"Sure," said Autumn a bit shyly. "I have noticed that they don't look

anything like the trees around me. I can shake them off if I want."

"Really?" said Skippy. "If I pull one off, will it hurt?"

"Go ahead, it won't hurt at all!" said Autumn.

"Wow!" exclaimed Skippy, "They pull off really easy and are nice to

touch, so soft and flexible. Not like the evergreen with their spikes. You

really have a good thing going here Autumn. May I pull out one more? I

really like the texture of them!"

"Pull out as many as you want! I have plenty." said Autumn, with a little

giggle. "It doesn't hurt at all."

"Gee, thanks, Autumn. Well, we know they're not needles, maybe we should name these too! Hey! I've got it! We'll call them May Pulls because you are so nice about saying I may pull them out," said Skippy with a smile.

" I want to take one more before I leave. Hey! That's it.....we'll call them, May Pull Leaves! There, now you are an official tree with an actual name for your cover up. You are Autumn with, let's shorten this to Maple Leaves. None of that prickly needle stuff for you....uh uh, you are way too good for that." Autumn just laughed. She didn't care what he named anything; It was just so good to have someone to talk to.

"I must say," said Autumn, "I do think I feel much better. It's so nice to have you to talk with Skippy, and I don't mind if you want to run around on me because it won't hurt at all! Make my limbs your playground anytime." Skippy began to jump from limb to limb on Autumn.

"Wow!" he exclaimed, "You have the nicest limbs I have ever been on!"

"Oh, you don't have to say that," Autumn said a little embarrassed. "I know how ugly I really am."

"Well, I'm not going to lie to you Kid," said Skippy, "You're not the best looking tree I have ever seen but you are definitely not a weed. Why...your branches and limbs are so wide and sturdy and long, just look at the way they bump and curve. You are built absolutely perfect for birds and

squirrels. Ya know, living here with you could be the best home that any of

us has ever had! I mean, just your Maple Leaves would give us a lot more

protection than anything we live in now. Not to mention we wouldn't get

soaked in the rain with them to protect us."

"You're just saying that," said Autumn, "You're being so nice to me."

 "Boy, you really are a newbie aren't you? You have a lot to learn Kid."

said Skippy.

Autumn continued, "But I know you and the other creatures in the

forest won't want to be seen living with such an ugly thing as me."

"When it comes to building homes there isn't an animal in the forest that

will let your strange looks stand in its way. Come on Autumn, what do ya

say? Can I spread the word? Are you willing to be a shelter for us?" Skippy

asked excitedly.

 " Well, well of course...if...if you really mean it. I've been alone for

such a long time, it would be wonderful to have the company, and I love

the thought of maybe doing something good. It would at least give me a

reason for being! I mean, it would be sort of like I was helping the animals

would't it?" Autumn asked softly.   "You bet it would!" stated Skippy.

DRAW OR PASTE A PICTURE OF SKIPPY

"You're going to be the best home any of us ever had, and when Winter

comes and the old Wind has a bad day, I'll bet you can help us to not

lose our nests...you really are just perfect for a home."

With that, Autumn began to feel something she had never felt before...

HAPPINESS!

"Oh, my goodness! " she exclaimed. "I'm going to have friends! I'm going

to be of use to someone! You go get everyone Skippy. I will get myself

arranged as best I can to accommodate all who would like to participate."

It wasn't very long before Skippy was introducing all the squirrels and birds

in the area to Autumn. She had found herself the best friend she could

ever have hoped for. Before Skippy was done, he would have the whole

forest living with her.

When Skippy's friends first saw her, they were naturally a little

skeptical because she definitely didn't look like any tree they had ever

seen. However, after a brief conversation with her, they could tell she was

just as sweet as sugar. Before long they began to make their homes with

Autumn . They could be heard remarking on how comfortable her branches

were, so wide and strong. She was perfect for whatever type of dwelling the animals wanted for their home. They found themselves feeling very proud to have such a wonderful place to live. It was no time at all before they forgot how strange Autumn looked as they focused on her gentle, kind manner. Never again did they think she was anything but wonderful.

Autumn's beauty was beginning to show, not in her appearance, but in her actions. If there was any way she could change anything to make one of her new roommates more comfortable, she did it without hesitation. She was so much happier now that she had company, and they really seemed to like her. There was always someone to talk to or a storm to get ready for. She took her job of protecting her friends very seriously. She almost didn't have time to feel badly about the evergreens ignoring her... almost.

News of the new home that the Birds and Squirrels had found traveled quickly. Soon wildlife from everywhere throughout the forest were coming to see this unusual tree. Many of them stayed...some made their home with Autumn while others made homes within the forest near by. Most of them who made the journey found the atmosphere so pleasant around Autumn that they wanted to remain close by. She actually had become quite famous...not as an ugly tree, but as a wonderful shelter. Not only did she house the animals, she often helped resolve the arguments among

them. She had developed the reputation of being very intelligent and fair.

**DRAW OR PASTE A PICTURE OF
YOUR MAPLE TREE WITH LEAVES AND BIRD NESTS**

As the time passed, Autumn continued to grow and grow, thus
housing more and more animals. Flowers even began to move into the
forest. There were only a few at first, then suddenly they were
everywhere! It was a lovely sight to behold, so much color and beauty.
The Butterflies came and different types of animals were moving in.
There were Wolves, Foxes, Bears, and Deer. There was no end to the
different species of birds that kept coming season after season.

There was even a couple of Parrots from down south! They stayed for
one season in the North Woods. They thanked Autumn and told her she
was great, but the winter wasn't, and they headed back to Florida. They
invited the birds to consider coming south for the winter if it got too cold.
When they arrived back to their home and told of what they saw, the
Crocodiles were amazed! No one had seen a tree like that or so many
animals together in one place, all getting along just fine. It was the talk
throughout the southern woods for a very long time. Many of the
southern animals made a trip in the summer just to see for themselves and
to meet Autumn.

The great forest was alive as never before. Even the Wind would not
just blow by. He would slow down to a gentle breeze and spend time

admiring the view. He was heard telling the Balsam that he had never in all his travels seen such a wonderful place. The Balsam was said to have answered, "Well naturally, we wouldn't have it any another way. We are, of course, the finest Forest in the land." The Wind agreed, and the evergreens became even more stuck up (if that was possible).

Most of Autumn's days were happy with lots of things to do, yet she still had this longing inside to have a tree like herself to talk with. She needed tree that would understand what she was feeling. The animals just didn't know.

When visiting with Mr. Owl she told him how her sap was getting thick when it began to get cool at night and that she couldn't move as easily when this happened.

"Tut tut, I have a touch of rheumatism in my back." responded Mr. Owl, "I know what you mean Dearie. Just take it easy for a day or two and you'll feel better." He didn't understand how much she hurt. That was when she realized no matter how many friends she had, no matter how great they all were, and as understanding as they tried to be, there wasn't one of them that could really understand how she felt, or how lonely she was sometimes.

Even Skippy who had become her very best friend over time, just didn't understand what it was like to be a tree like none other. He suggested that she eat better because he thought that might make a difference. They spent many hours talking. Skippy had taught her so much about those parts of the forest she had never seen. Autumn loved their long conversations. He always made her laugh and let her know how much he cared about her. Skippy had recently fallen in love and brought his mate to meet Autumn. She could see that he was genuinely happy but she had never seen him behave so awkwardly! As happy for Skippy as she was, it served to remind her of how lonely she felt. She was, in fact, the only one in the great forest that did not have a partner.

A few years ago she had become very excited when Skippy told her that the influx of new animals and birds had brought new species of trees into the great evergreen forest; and they were sprouting up everywhere! She asked the birds and animals to please keep watch for trees that looked like her. Skippy told every living thing about Autumn's request and each day asked that a report be given to Autumn. It had become a routine for all the animals, as soon as they returned from their travels, to go and talk with Autumn about what they had seen and the new trees they had met.

They told her of ones with white bark, some with leaves that looked a little

like hers but the bark was very different, and about some that grew

wonderful nuts that were shared with the animals, adding to their food

source. The forest was becoming more interesting with each passing

season, but no trees were ever found that were the same as Autumn. She

was longing more and more for the company of a tree like herself, and had

all but given up hope of ever finding it. She decided she truly was just an

ugly mistake.

She did, however, feel lucky to have all the friends and company that

she had. Though she was still the only one in the forest that didn't have

someone like herself to spend time with, she laughed with one of her

roommates each and every day. It wasn't that she didn't love her life. It

was just hard not having someone that totally understood her.

The years passed and Autumn kept growing. Each spring more homes

could be found among her broad strong limbs. Her reputation brought all

sorts of forest life from very far places. Autumn was so accommodating to

their housing needs. Even those who chose to house elsewhere still loved

spending time with Autumn. At the first sign of cold weather, she tucked

DRAW OR PAST A PICTURE OF
YOUR FOREST FLOOR WITH FLOWERS AND BUTTERFLIES

all her Maple Leaves around the nest and kept her friends safe and warm.

After all this time the evergreens still couldn't figure Autumn out. She was

so highly regarded in the forest that they couldn't openly criticize her. The

last time one of the Pine trees had made a nasty comment about her, a

flock of birds and a bunch of squirrels had made a real mess of the tree.

That was all it took, (Being covered with a white mess was NOT socially

acceptable). Autumn would hear them whispering amongst themselves but

she couldn't make out what they said. They still, after all these years, had

never spoken a word to her. Nor did they socialize with any of the other

species of trees that were growing amongst them. They were just acting

 so superior. The new trees were able to keep company among themselves

so they didn't care. There were a few close enough to speak with Autumn.

Once in a while one would 'holler' a "Good Morning," but Autumn wasn't

comfortable yelling back so it wasn't really a visit.

The Spruce did say something one day that was almost a compliment.

   " Well," addressing the other evergreens, "aren't you glad we didn't get

rid of the weed?"

Autumn couldn't believe her ears. Was the Spruce really going to says

something kind about her? The Spruce continued, "She is just perfect for housing the animals so we haven't been bothered putting up with that mess for years. Ahhh, such freedom! She has helped to bring attention to our beauty. We now have many visitors and they can't help but see how lovely we are in comparison. I think she really has served us well. I am sure that's the reason she was put here. Remind me to thank the Wind for bringing her."

Autumn should have known, they would never accept her as more than something that made them look better. She felt so sad. A few of the Birds saw the affect that the words of the Spruce had on Autumn. In retaliation, they decided to do a 'white flyover'. When they were done, the Spruce looked like it had been through a snow storm! Autumn tried not to giggle when she saw it, but the Spruce was screaming and yelling and insisting they stop. It kept trying to move, but to no avail. The whole thing sounded and looked so funny that she just could not help giggling. Then, suddenly she felt bad for the Spruce. She knew what it was like to be made fun of. She talked with the Birds and told them that she appreciated their sticking up for her but she really didn't want them to embarrass the evergreens. She just wasn't comfortable with it. Revenge just didn't bring her any pleasure. The Birds had a really good time and felt the tree deserved it and more, but they would respect Autumn's wishes and not do

it again. Autumn wasn't going to let the evergreen's unkindness change

who she was. She remained as sweet as ever. She continued to do her

best to provide safe and warm homes for her little friends.

The great Balsam had heard Autumn speak to the Birds and he couldn't

help but admire her acceptance and kind attitude. A spark of respect and

appreciation for Autumn began to grow in him. She truly was a unique tree

in many regards. However, he said not a word.

**DRAW OR PASTE A PICTURE OF
YOUR BIRDS FLYING OVER THE ONE EVERGREEN AND
LEAVING IT A WHITE MESS**

Another two seasons passed without incident. When the chill in the air

was the warning of winter approaching, Autumn asked Skippy to speak

with her privately. "Skippy, there is something I have been thinking about.

I am not as strong as I used to be, and I really don't feel as good as I used

to. I think when you told me to eat better you were right,"

she chuckled. "You and our friends are so wonderful and it feels so good to

know that I have helped you all with housing. However, I have decided to

make a change. I have been thinking about it since you explained how the

trees had multiplied.

   "Wow!" exclaimed Skippy, "That was ages ago...so what have you been

pondering?"

   Autumn continued, "When the cold weather comes this year I am going

to ask the Wind to take my Maple Leaves and carry them all over the forest.

I will attach what I will call my 'SPINNERS' to many of the leaves. They

will contain seeds that I have been saving for a very long time. I hope they

will allow me to procreate."

   "What!" Skippy exclaimed in alarm, "Kid, (after all this time he still

called her Kid, and that made her smile.) I always knew you were

different, but I sure never thought you were crazy! What's the matter with you? No tree has ever done that!"

"Skippy, will you please listen to what I'm saying? I want you and

the others to start looking for new homes that will keep you safe all

winter. Maybe, the birds should consider the invitation made by Parrots to

go south for a few months. Once you have all moved out, I will dress in my

very best colors. Since I have never done that before, it will be fun! Then, I

will ask the Wind take my leaves, with 'spinners' attached, all over the

forest. Hopefully, in the spring, little trees like me will begin to grow. Then

you and the other animals will have room to spread out. You will be able to

live in any part of the forest you like. Also, I will have trees like me to

spend time with. I just don't want to be the only tree in the forest with

Maple Leaves. Not that you won't still be my very best friend! I mean I love

you Skippy,...but I would like to share feelings with someone

that truly knows how I feel. I will bring some trees like myself into the

forest. They will never be lonely and just think how the evergreens will

feel!" With that they both began to laugh. "So please Skippy, spread the

word to all our friends so they will look for safe shelter elsewhere this

winter."

"Gee Kid", said Skippy "I didn't realize that you were so lonely . I'm not as good a friend as I should have been...I never thought about how happy I

am with a family and that you really don't have one. Hope you can forgive

my being so self centered. I hate this idea though. Isn't there anything I

can do to change your mind?"

"Skippy, you are a wonderful friend. If I were a squirrel, I'm sure I

wouldn't need anyone but you to spend time with because you're great

company! Really, I love our time together!" Autumn reassured him, " There

is one thing you can do for me, however. Please promise me, if I don't wake

up in the spring, and you see the trees like me begin to grow , please tell

them that they are Maple Trees? Please spell it that way M A P L E, let

them know that they can be proud of themselves. They are unique,

but not alone."

"I promise, I will do that, but let's not talk about it...you will be fine,

a bit chilled, but fine. You just hold on to that thought... we WILL be

together again in the spring! I'll be moving my stuff back in because we're

roomies for life. (sniff) Please get this (sniff) out of your system once and

for all." Skippy said this with as much self assurance as he could, but

Autumn heard the apprehension he was feeling in his heart. No tree had

ever let their leaves go before. Who knew how this would turn out?

"Skippy, please don't cry, I need to do this regardless of the outcome. It's what I'm here to do and I couldn't feel better about it. I need you to celebrate it with me. I will miss you all and will really look forward to spring and our reunion."

"Heck no, I'm not crying!....okay, maybe just a little. I really do understand, Autumn, I just don't like it." Skippy said through his sniffling. "I really wish I could talk you out of this. I wish you would listen to me! But I have known you long enough to know there is no sense in arguing. I will do what you have asked, but I won't really like it!" With that, Skippy slowly began to climb up Autumn's trunk to tell the others what her plans were and that they had to move. Autumn called after him.

" Thank you Skippy, you are a wonderful friend, and you have helped me in so many ways. I will think of you often this winter and will look forward to seeing you in the spring with all your belongings, ready to move back in." Autumn was smiling.

The fall was upon them. The animals were very busy finding new homes and moving. They all thanked Autumn for the wonderful time they had spent living with her. Some of them tried on several different occasions to talk her out of it. Mr. Owl and several Birds tried. Mr. Bear talked with her but she had made up her mind. There would be no changing it. They ended

up wishing her well and said they looked forward to coming back. Skippy

was the last to leave with his family. It was a teary good-by for them all .

They kept it short, with Autumn reiterating her request, in case things

didn't go as planned, and Skippy promising to honor it. Surely it wouldn't

be necessary. Then there was a long hug. Skippy turned and walked away

but stopped to wave one last time. Autumn waved one of her giant

branches. It was rather impressive if she did say so herself. "Good

Heavens" she thought, "Was she getting egotistical through osmosis? She

sure hoped not."

DRAW OR PASTE A PICTURE OF
YOUR ANIMALS LEAVING THEIR HOME WITH AUTUMN

"Oh," said Autumn after they had all left, "it's so quiet! I hope they are all going to be all right. I shall miss them so very much." For just a moment, she was having second thoughts. Maybe she should not do this? No, she had to! With mixed emotions, Autumn started to dress in her most beautiful leaf colors. By the time Fall was turning cold, she was the most spectacular tree in the entire forest. As a matter of fact, rumor had it that never had the Wind in all his travels, or anyone else, seen such splendor! Her leaves ranged in color from exquisite Gold , to deep Red, bright Orange and deep Purple with a mix of everything in between. Many animals that had heard of her but had never seen her, came and marveled at her overwhelming beauty. Autumn being Autumn, didn't let any of the compliments go to her head. She appreciated being called nice things and being told she was, by far, the most wonderful tree ever seen. She wanted very much to make sure her offspring would have every advantage in their lives, and she felt this was giving them a good start. Not for herself did she dress, it was for them.

It was almost winter. The Wind had agreed to come by and take her leaves with the spinners as far as he could, dropping them along the forest floor. She was sure that would be any day now. It was on a particularly crisp day when Autumn heard someone calling her name. It was a voice she thought she recognized, but wasn't sure.

"Autumn, Autumn....I can understand if you choose to ignore me. I deserve that, having ignored you all these years." It was the Great Balsam. Autumn was so stunned that he was speaking to her that she couldn't answer for a full minute.

"Oh my, no, please forgive me! I just didn't expect that you would be talking to ME! I was stunned into silence!"

"Forgive you? Autumn, please...forgive me, though I don't deserve your forgiveness. I have watched and listened to you these many years and never have I heard an unkind word from you. No matter how badly you were treated, or how harsh our words were, you remained kind and held fast to your standard. Obviously, one that is much better than ours. I heard you chastise the Birds that time they served up 'white out' on the Spruce," he said with a chuckle. "I must admit it was deserved. I now realize we all underestimated you from the time we chose to call you a 'weed' until just recently. I know I can't make up for our unkindness and the pain it so unnecessarily caused you. Please know from this day forth, when any of us speak to you, or of you, it will be with the utmost respect.

We now know you are, by far, the finest most excellent and beautiful tree in the forest. I bow to you, Autumn." The Great Balsam allowed all of his limbs to hang long and low as he leaned forward to honor her. The rest of the evergreens seeing this, all in order, did the same. "I believe what you have done in the past, and are doing now, is an exceptional display of kindness and generosity," expressed the Great Balsam. "You put us to shame. You have my total respect and admiration. I hope we can have long conversations in the spring. I will look forward to that."

" Oh, I don't know what to say, I have always been in awe of you...I am so glad we can talk a bit, I too, would like to get to know you and all the others. I will be so grateful to have your company in the spring!" said Autumn without hesitation.

"You are, too kind Autumn; we don't deserve that, but I'm happy that we might have the privilege of being exposed to your kindness. Maybe you can teach us more about humility. I think we have forgotten some of the basics." stated the Great Balsam.

" I, I am embarrassed," Autumn said shyly. " I don't deserve all your praise. I am just the ugly tree in the forest. I so much appreciate your acknowledging me at all! You really are magnificent to look at, but you know that."

" Ah, sweet Autumn, " said the Great Balsam. " I look at you in all your splendor, and I will leave you with this. Your beauty, both inner and outer, is unsurpassed. Being your magnificent self is closer to perfection than most of us could hope to achieve in a lifetime. Autumn, you don't have to change a thing... It's the rest of us that need to do some changing."
The other evergreens, out of embarrassment all agreed and one at a time apologized to Autumn for their disrespect. They made a promise to Autumn to spend time in the spring working on friendships. She finally had the respect of the evergreens and did appreciate it, but they still weren't her kind of tree. They also commented without end about how beautiful she looked, but it didn't change her need for a tree like herself.

Now, unbeknown to Autumn, Skippy had heard the entire conversation. He had moved into one of the Pines right nearby. He wanted to be close in case she needed him. The word was soon spread throughout the forest about the conversation between Autumn and the evergreens. The Butterflies were so happy that they delayed their departure and swarmed throughout the forest kissing all the trees. Even though winter was almost upon them and it meant getting a bit chilly, the Birds sang and the Squirrels chattered away. It was a cause for celebration; Their Autumn single handedly united the entire forest. The Birds gave their word that they would not do the 'white out' on the evergreens anymore (which was very well received). Autumn, too ,was grateful for a wonderful life full of good friends and to be living in a forest full of love. Some were in hopes, that given the new circumstances, she might change her mind about this whole reproduction thing. Autumn, as happy as she was, still longed for her own soul mate. So, with even more resolve, she prepared for the winter.

DRAW OR PASTE A PICURE OF
AUTUMN SPEAKING WITH THE GREAT BALSAM

DRAW YOUR MAPLE TREE WITH NO LEAVES AND SNOW ON ITS' BRANCHES

The days were getting chilly and Autumn knew the time was close. Soon the Wind stopped by as he promised he would, and he blew and blew until he had removed the very last of Autumn's leaves and spinners. He carried them throughout the forest as he had promised he would, creating a beautiful forest floor. He told all he came across that he felt honored to have been chosen for the task. When he reported back to Autumn, he told her he even tried to place a leaf on the top of the spinners to protect them. It was a job well done. Autumn finally relaxed believing in her goal.

Shortly thereafter, the winter began in earnest. It was the coldest, snowiest winter that had ever been seen in the great forest. Even the evergreen trees were huddled together, for they, too, were freezing. Autumn stood alone with no leaves to protect her and no heat from animal nests to warm her. She made not a sound except a little cough now and then. Never did she complain about the cold. Several of the animals who lived nearby checked on her from time to time. Then the snow became too deep and they were kept away. In the middle of one of the most horrible storms she was heard to give out a long sigh...it was the last sound anyone heard from her. As hard as she tried, she just could no longer endure the cold. As she was resting she entered her eternal sleep. She did so happily, knowing that she, Autumn, the ugliest tree in the forest, had made a difference. No one would ever be alone, and no one would ever again think her offspring were ugly. She knew she had made more homes for he friends and their families. Yes, Autumn did die. She passed peacefully, feeling good about who she was and what she had accomplished.

The winter finally gave way to spring and the snow began to melt in the valleys. The sun became warmer and melted the ice from the evergreens. The Birds, Squirrels, and other forest wildlife began cleaning out their winter homes. It had been a tough winter and they had really missed the shelter that Autumn had given them for so long. Skippy was the first to arrive but all of her former tenants were making their way back to her. As they traveled, it was obvious that Autumn's plan had worked. All over the great forest, small trees that looked like Autumn were beginning to sprout everywhere. They were already talking with everyone and asking all kinds of questions. The Spruce and Pines were laughing with them and telling them tales about the forest. Skippy began jumping from evergreen to evergreen. He just wanted to get to Autumn and let her know, if she didn't already, that her plan had worked! He was leaping onto a spruce when he saw her - it was obvious that she had succumbed to the cold.

Skippy was devastated.

"THIS IS NOT FAIR!!!" he yelled at the top of his lungs. " She did it! It worked! She should be here to see it!"

"Who is She? Who are you? What did She do?" asked a little voice that sounded so much like Autumn did when they had first met that Skippy was startled. It was a little tree, and to Skippy it really was a cute little thing.

"Why, I'm Skippy, and She was Autumn. You have her to thank for being here." he said. He looked around and saw more and more of the little ones, all of them reflecting the beauty that Skippy had come to know in Autumn.

"Hello Skippy. It's nice to know that Autumn made us! Where is she? I want to thank her, that was so nice of her and, she gave me a bunch of friends!" said one little tree happily.

"Hello", all the little trees cried out in bubbly little voices. "Will you tell Autumn thank you from us, too She must be very special!"

Skippy got a kick out of the way they said Autumn, they couldn't really pronounce it correctly but it sounded cute. Skippy knew Autumn would have gotten a chuckle out of it so he let it be.

DRAW OR PASTE A PICTURE OF
SKIPPY TALKING TO ALL THE LITTLE MAPLE TREES

"You can't even imagine, she was the most fantastic tree in the entire forest," said Skippy.

"What do you mean was?" asked one of the little trees.

Skippy took a deep breath and let it out. " Listen closely, I have a story to tell you and I want you to pass it on to the Birds and other animals so they can tell the rest of the trees like you how they came to be. This won't be easy for me because she was my best friend, so if I get a little choked up, I hope you'll understand."

" We really would like to know, but we don't want to make you sad," said the little tree that reminded Skippy of Autumn . Skippy could not believe how much like her they all were. They even appeared to have her kind soul. Then he remembered the promise he had made to Autumn; to tell the little ones about her if she didn't make it.

"Okay, listen up! This is how you came to be. Autumn decided to let all of her leaves blow off and take her spinners (those are the things she put her seeds in that would create you guys). You see, there was no other tree in the entire forest that was like her. She did all this great stuff for everyone else so we could have safe warm places to live and raise our families. She had no family of her own, so she was really alone with no one to really understand how she was feeling. She told me she wanted a soul

mate. Single handedly, she changed the forest from a place of just

evergreens, to a place filled with different trees, flowers, and animals.

Why, by all accounts, she brought about changes that made this the

grandest forest in the country! She did it all without even knowing it was

her beautiful spirit that brought about all the great changes. She was the

kindest and most thoughtful friend any of us could ever have had (sniff)

and we will all miss her very much." Skippy blew his nose and continued.

"I wish you could have heard the ridiculous disagreements some of us had,

and how Autumn would listen so patiently to both sides and come up with a

simple solution that made everyone happy. Anyway, she was amazing!

This past fall she decided not to be lonely anymore. She dressed in her

most beautiful leaves, sent out her spinners, and here you are. She was

really something to see, I'll tell ya, she was just beautiful! A fine idea it

was, except that she had no way of knowing that the winter would be the

fiercest ever in the history of the forest. I'm afraid as much as she wanted

to be here to spend time with you, it was just too cold and she went to

sleep." Gosh! This was the most difficult thing Skippy had ever had to do,

but he had to do it...he had promised Autumn. So, being Skippy, he couldn't stop there. He told them about how Autumn had been shunned by all

the other trees in the forest because she did not look like them. Then he

told them about how her loneliness just continued to grow over the years

until she made this decision.

"You should have seen her!" he continued, "All the animals far and wide

would come just to look at her because she was a wonder and inspiration

to us all. Even the great Wind paid his respects and he never stopped to

talk to anyone. Probably the best part was that all the evergreens told her

how sorry they were to have been so unkind for all those many seasons.

They asked her to forgive them and paid her great compliments on all her

actions. It was a beautiful for all in the forest. Oh, that reminds

me...she asked me to tell you that you are to be known as Maple Trees.

Remind me to tell you why one day." Skippy smiled as he remembered

pulling off Autumn's leaves.

All the little trees began whispering among themselves. The one that

sounded and looked the most like Autumn said, "We have made a decision.

We are going to grow proud and strong. We will be the best Maple Trees

anyone can find anywhere. We will make homes for all the animals

throughout the spring, summer and fall, but just before winter, we will dress in our loveliest colors to honor our mother. Then, we too, will let our

leaves blow all over the forest so she can continue forever. All the forest

will remember her until the end of time.

Autumn, the one that changed the color of the forest!

"Wow!" exclaimed Skippy, "That will be wonderful! But we will have to

remember to feed you really well so you stay warm in the winter. Your

mother never did eat right…You leave that to me, I will make sure you

have plenty of food and fun." Skippy was elated! Autumn would continue

forever. It was the next best thing to having her. He was so happy that he

did something he hadn't done since the day he met Autumn. He bounded

through the evergreens but instead of complaining, the whole forest

laughed and helped bounce him around. Yes, the forest had really changed.

"Could I have your attention, please?" said a loud, commanding voice. It

was the Great Balsam. "First, I would like to welcome all you young trees

to the forest. You can make your home anywhere you like, we are happy to

move over to accommodate you." He especially liked the little tree that

sounded like Autumn. "I shall call you Little Autumn, and I ask you to stay

by me if you don't mind. I will teach you how to live in the forest the way

that your mother taught me, and you can pass that knowledge on to your brothers and sisters. So I make this 'decree' to be spread through all the

forest. The Fall of the year from now on will be called "Autumn" in honor

of the Maple Tree that changed the forest. These young trees will let us

know by changing their leaf color when Autumn begins, and it shall be a

time of celebration and sharing in the forest, of helping the animals

secure themselves for the winter and simply enjoy each other's company."

All the trees were in agreement. It was a wonderful day in the forest.

Skippy then bounded off to tell all the forest of the 'decree' made by the

Balsam. It was truly a day of tribute and honor to Autumn that would

continue forevermore. And so it was, and has been from that time...in the

fall of the year, the Maple Trees put on their most beautiful leaves and, in

memory of the tree that gave everything, that season will always be known

throughout the entire world as AUTUMN.

THE END

**DRAW OR PASTE A PICTURE OF
HOW "THE STORY OF AUTUMN" MAKES YOU FEEL**

CONGRATULATIONS TO_____

YOU HAVE CREATED A ONE OF A KIND BOOK WITH YOUR PERSONAL PICTURES AND OR DRAWINGS. THERE ISN'T AN OTHER ONE JUST LIKE THIS ONE IN THE WHOLE WORLD!

YOUR NEW WORDS PAGE 1

WORD   **DEFINITION**

_____

_____

_____

_____

_____

_____

_____

_____

_____

_____

_____

_____

_____

_____

_____

_____

_____

_____

_____

_____

_____

_____

_____

YOUR NEW WORDS PAGE 2

WORD   **DEFINITION**

CPSIA information can be obtained
at www.ICGtesting.com
Printed in the USA
BVHW01*1253140518
516190BV00003B/5/P